This Ladybird Book belongs to:

_____

_____

_____

_____

retold by Joan Stimson
illustrated by Petula Stone

Cover illustration by John Gurney

Originally published in the United Kingdom by Ladybird Books Ltd © 1993

First American edition by Ladybird Books USA
An Imprint of Penguin USA Inc.
375 Hudson Street, New York, New York 10014

Printed in Great Britain
10 9 8 7 6 5 4 3 2 1

ISBN 0-7214-5649-9

FAVORITE TALES

Chicken
Licken

nce upon a time, there was a little chick called Chicken Licken. One day, as he was eating under an oak tree, an acorn fell on his head.

"Yikes!" cried Chicken Licken.
"The sky is falling! The sky is falling!"

And he ran off to tell the King.

On the way, Chicken Licken met Henny Penny. "Oh! Henny Penny!" Chicken Licken cried. "The sky is falling! The sky is falling! I'm off to tell the King."

"That's awful!" said Henny Penny. "I shall come, too!"

So Chicken Licken and Henny Penny hurried off to find the King.

On the way, Chicken Licken and
Henny Penny met Cocky Locky.

"Oh! Cocky Locky!" Chicken Licken cried.

"The sky is falling! The sky is falling! We're off to tell the King!"

"Dreadful news!" replied Cocky Locky. "I shall come, too!"

So Chicken Licken, Henny Penny, and Cocky Locky hurried off to find the King.

On the way, Chicken Licken, Henny Penny, and Cocky Locky met Ducky Lucky.

"Oh! Ducky Lucky!" cried Chicken Licken. "The sky is falling! The sky is falling! We're off to tell the King."

"How scary!" said Ducky Lucky. "I shall come, too."

So Chicken Licken, Henny Penny,
Cocky Locky, and Ducky Lucky
hurried off to find the King.

On the way, Chicken Licken, Henny Penny, Cocky Locky, and Ducky Lucky met Drakey Lakey.

"Oh! Drakey Lakey!" cried Chicken Licken. "The sky is falling! The sky is falling! We're off to tell the King."

"Most frightening!" agreed Drakey Lakey. "I shall come, too."

So Chicken Licken, Henny Penny, Cocky Locky, Ducky Lucky, and Drakey Lakey hurried off to find the King.

On the way, Chicken Licken, Henny Penny, Cocky Locky, Ducky Lucky, and Drakey Lakey met Goosey Loosey.

"Oh! Goosey Loosey!" cried Chicken Licken. "The sky is falling! The sky is falling! We're off to tell the King."

"What a catastrophe!" said Goosey Loosey. "I shall come, too!"

So Chicken Licken, Henny Penny,
Cocky Locky, Ducky Lucky, Drakey Lakey,
and Goosey Loosey hurried off to find
the King.

On the way, Chicken Licken, Henny Penny, Cocky Locky, Ducky Lucky, Drakey Lakey, and Goosey Loosey met Turkey Lurkey.

"Oh! Turkey Lurkey!" cried Chicken Licken. "The sky is falling! The sky is falling! We're off to tell the King."

"Good gracious!" said Turkey Lurkey. "I shall come, too."

So Chicken Licken, Henny Penny,
Cocky Locky, Ducky Lucky,
Drakey Lakey, Goosey Loosey,
and Turkey Lurkey hurried off
to find the King.

But on the way, they met Foxy Loxy!

"Good morning," said Foxy Loxy.
"Where are you all going in such a hurry?"

"Oh! Foxy Loxy!" cried Chicken Licken.
"The sky is falling! The sky is falling!
We're off to tell the King."

"Follow me," said Foxy Loxy. "I'll show you a shortcut to the King's castle."

So Chicken Licken, Henny Penny, Cocky Locky, Ducky Lucky, Drakey Lakey, Goosey Loosey, and Turkey Lurkey followed Foxy Loxy.

But instead of taking them to the King,
Foxy Loxy led them straight to his den,
where his wife and three children were
waiting for their supper.

They were *very* hungry.

The hungry foxes quickly gobbled up
Chicken Licken, Henny Penny, Cocky
Locky, Ducky Lucky, Drakey Lakey,
Goosey Loosey, and Turkey Lurkey.

So Chicken Licken and his friends
never did warn the King that the sky
was falling.

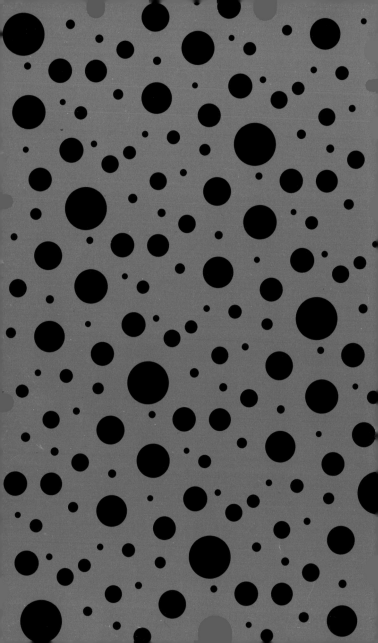